ONE OF THOSE GLAZE

RAISED AND GLAZED COZY MYSTERIES,
BOOK 19

EMMA AINSLEY

SUMMER PRESCOTT BOOKS PUBLISHING

CHAPTER ONE

"I can't believe you're buying another outfit for that baby," Ruby Cobb said to her best friend, Maggie Sharpe. They walked slowly, each pushing a cart through the department store after their trip to the restaurant supply store in Joplin.

"I'm not just buying something else for 'that baby,'" Maggie said. "I have two outfits in there, one for the new baby and one for Wyatt."

"So, it's justified as long as you buy one for Myra's baby and one for your grandson?"

"Absolutely." Maggie grinned. She set two more toys in her cart and pushed it through the store.

"You're out of control," Ruby said when they loaded their packages into the back of Maggie's car.

"I might well be," Maggie said. She climbed into

the driver's seat and headed for the highway. The plan was to stop by the new donut shop location in Hunter Springs before they headed back to Dogwood Mountain.

Although the new donut shop had been up and running for a few weeks, the official grand opening was slated for the coming week. Maggie and Ruby had made the trip to Joplin for a few more supplies for the festivities. Ruby had suggested they make a stop to pick up the banners and grand opening coupons from the printer directly, so they could be sure to receive the correct items.

"They turned out well," Ruby said as she turned one of the cards over in her hand. "I like the picture of the old filling station illuminated at dusk on the front."

"That was Bradley's idea," Maggie said.

"I hear a little bit of pride in your voice there, Mama," Ruby said gently. "And you should be proud. For him to take on such a leadership role with the new location with no experience is remarkable."

"Sometimes I wonder if that's due to his experience in the Navy, or just his instincts," Maggie said.

"If I had to guess, I'd have to say it's a little bit of both," Ruby said. She pushed the card back into the box with the rest of them and carefully set the box on the backseat. "By the way, have you spoken with Brett much lately?"

Maggie shook her head and turned toward the exit for Hunter Springs. "I have not, actually," she said. "Since the special election that made him sheriff, he's been working about fourteen hours a day."

"I think Chief Macklin has been about as busy," Ruby said. "I wonder if Brooks is going to regret this promotion to police chief after the baby is born."

"I don't know, but I'm really glad the change was made now and not after she's born," Maggie said. "Can you imagine a new baby and a new job change? All at the same time?"

"No, that is one scenario I cannot imagine," Ruby admitted.

"Oh, Ruby. I didn't mean anything by that," Maggie said quickly. She felt her face redden slightly at the mention of her friend's childless state.

"It's alright," Ruby said softly. "I made a lot of choices in my life and one of them was to pursue my culinary career."

"You never considered children?" Maggie asked her. They'd really never discussed it before.

Ruby nodded her head. "I did, and I even tried to have a child, for a short time," she said.

"I never knew that."

"I don't ever talk about it because, as you can plainly see, I was not successful in that endeavor," Ruby said matter-of-factly.

Questions filled her mind, but she kept them to herself. If Ruby wanted to share more, she would when she was ready. Maggie drove through the residential neighborhoods in Hunter Springs before she pulled into the old downtown business area and parked in front of what had been a filling station, but was now the new location of the second donut shop.

"The sign looks good," she said. A discussion had occurred between Bradley, Ruby, and herself to amplify the natural rustic industrial aesthetic of the building. The result was a metal cut-out sign backlit against a reclaimed wood background. The dark, earthy tones in the wood set off the black metal sign in the best ways.

"I like that we kept the name simple," Ruby said. "'Hunter Springs Donut Shop.'"

"I agree," Maggie said. "For a moment, I thought we might do something a little more creative."

"But if it ain't broke, don't fix it," Ruby said with a smile.

"Something like that," Maggie agreed. "I think we'd better get these things inside and head back to Dogwood Mountain."

Ruby agreed. She grabbed the bags from the backseat and headed for the front door of the donut shop. "Where do we want to put this stuff?"

Bradley stood behind the wood-topped counter. "If that's more for the grand opening, just put everything in the office for now."

"Gotcha," Ruby said. "Oh, and your mother did a little bit of shopping for the small fries."

Bradley's face fell. "Seriously," he said. "I'm going to have to buy a second house just to store everything she's bought for Wyatt."

"It will slow down after Myra's baby gets here," Ruby said quietly. "She is just going a little nuts over the new baby coming, I think."

"You mean she has to buy something for Wyatt every time she buys something for the new baby?" Bradley asked.

"*She* is right behind you," Maggie said from behind Ruby. "And *she* is not the one who already bought an entire suite of baby furniture."

"That was supposed to be a secret," Ruby said.

Jake Jenkins, Maggie's young employee who opened the store with Bradley, emerged from the back carrying a tray of clean coffee mugs with him. "Did you tell him about the motorized truck you bought for Wyatt?"

Maggie and Bradley glanced at each other. "You bought him a motorized truck?" Bradley asked.

Ruby shrugged and ran her hand down the polished wood counter. "You know, I'm so glad you decided to get rid of the red paint in here. I like this rustic look a lot better."

"We got rid of it because the little handprints did more damage to it than we thought in the beginning," Maggie said, referring to the smallest member of the Sharpe family who had decided to help out in his own way while the old filling station was being remodeled into a donut shop. "And you are avoiding the accusation that was just laid at your feet. Have you or have you not purchased a motorized vehicle for a one-year-old child?"

"I know he won't be ready for this truck for a little while. But you have to see it, guys. It's a miniature Ford F-150. Shiny Black."

"It's a Ford." Bradley's eyes widened. "You actually bought him one of those?"

Ruby grinned. She pulled her phone out of her pocket and flipped through a half dozen photos of the truck she had taken out on her property. "And before you have anything to say, he can safely use it in town at your new house with the fenced back yard and at

Aunt Ruby's farm whenever you two get the itch to ride out on the open range."

"It's not a pony, for Pete's sake." Maggie smiled. She was ecstatic about the thought of her little grandson tearing around the yard in a lifelike truck. It was one of the many things she adored about being a grandmother rather than a mother. The thought of Bradley at his age in a motorized truck would have terrorized her. With age, she had learned to relax and enjoy life a little more.

"Hey, Mom," Bradley said, looking out the large front overhead windows that opened like garage doors.

"The sheriff just pulled up. My guess is that he's here to see you."

"Who else would he be here to see?" Ruby chuckled.

"Hey," Maggie said. "You're just happy that the attention is off you for a minute."

While they were chatting, Brett Mission climbed out of a black SUV with the county sheriff's department logo on the door.

"Hey, everyone," Brett said with a wave.

He made small talk with Bradley and Jake for a moment before he asked if he could speak with Maggie alone outside. She waved at Ruby, who had just started her pickup truck and was heading back to Dogwood Mountain.

"Is there something going on?" Maggie asked Brett when they were alone outside in the parking lot next to her car. "You seem a little bit off today."

"I just wanted to check in with you," Brett said. In the weeks since he had taken over as the county sheriff, his stress level seemed to have changed for the worse.

"Was there something specific you wanted to talk about?" Maggie asked him. Brett gazed off into the distance and sighed.

"I don't know, Maggie. You're going to think I'm crazy," he said. "But I want you to be careful."

"Be careful? Just in general?"

Brett nodded. His gaze shifted to her. "I've seen some disturbing reports around the county. And my first thought went to you," he said.

"What are these reports about?" Maggie asked. She felt her skin prickle under his gaze. "Can you at least tell me something... anything?"

"There have been five reports of women being followed this week alone," he said. "The reports have come in from all across the county, and the descriptions of the assailant have differed from case to case."

"The descriptions have differed?" Maggie raised a brow. "That's strange."

"The entire matter is strange. So far, the reports have all been called in, but nobody has agreed to speak to law enforcement in person. My gut tells me there's more to what's happening than we've been able to put together," Brett said. "I think we're going to find out that the cases are connected somehow, but we just haven't made the connection yet. We might be dealing with a possible serial offender, and I just want you to be careful."

"I'm always careful, but I will try harder to be more careful," she said. "Is there anything else I ought to know about this?"

"Just that the situations seem to be happening in isolated areas. One was a lady leaving work after a late night shift at a bar. Another was a woman who had pulled over on the side of the road when she thought she had a flat tire. We aren't sure if they're attempted abductions, a serial stalking, or someone just trying to scare people."

"Where exactly did all of these incidences take place?" Maggie asked.

"All over the county, really," Brett said. "But mainly in rural or small town areas. The times varied, but it was generally late at night or early in the morning."

"And it was always a different caller, but also a different driver?"

Brett shook his head. "Honestly, I'm not sure what's going on, but my gut instinct tells me that even if it isn't the same person each time, these attacks are related somehow."

Maggie moved in and approached Brett for a hug. She wrapped her arms quickly around his neck, squeezed, and then let him go. In that moment, her emotions overtook her. She was so touched by his concern and the time he took to express it. "Thank you."

He sighed and placed his hands on her shoulders. "I just want you to be safe."

"I'll do my best," Maggie said. She waved at Bradley, who had glanced out of the donut shop window, then climbed in her car and headed back home to Dogwood Mountain.

CHAPTER TWO

"Why don't you let me get that for you?" Maggie asked Myra Sawyer Macklin the following morning. It was early, just ten minutes after six, and Myra was seated on a stool at the baker's table where she had taken over Maggie's duties. Part of her duties included rolling out the cinnamon roll dough. For the third time inside an hour, the rolling pin had gone spinning off of the table and landed on the floor.

To retrieve it, Myra had to slide slowly off of her stool, push herself off of the table and stand over where the rolling pin had traveled. She then had to plant her feet as wide apart as she could and bend forward, all the while holding onto her swollen belly with one hand and reaching for the pin with the other.

"No, it's okay, Maggie," Myra said as she slipped off of the stool. "I've got it."

"No, you don't," Orson Hawley said from across the kitchen. "Get on back up where you were before I tie you to the thing. And you just sit where you are before that baby comes sliding out and smacks you in the head for not being more careful."

"I'll get it Orson," Maggie said and headed for the rolling pin, which had traveled all the way to the other side of the kitchen and stopped under the prep table.

"Just throw that one in the sink," Orson ordered. Ruby stood at the prep table and picked the rolling pin up herself. She glanced knowingly at Maggie. Orson, who himself had slowed down a bit in the past several months, made sure to see to the welfare of everyone at the donut shop. His attention was especially keen on Myra. After her marriage to Brooks Macklin, they had welcomed Orson into the mother-in-law suite in their first house together. Orson was also the closest thing to a father that Myra had ever had. He had even walked her down the aisle at her wedding.

Orson disappeared into the store room for a moment and when he returned, he carried two brand new wooden rolling pins, each with a half-inch hole drilled in the end of each handle. He carried two lengths of thick rope and a new apron.

"Take off that dirty apron," he ordered Myra. She stood and slipped the apron over her large stomach. "Put this one on and I'll thread the rope through each end."

Activity in the kitchen ceased as everyone turned to watch what Orson did next. He pushed the ends of one rope through the holes in the handles and tied a tight knot. He turned to Myra and fastened the other end of each rope to a loop on the waist of the new apron Myra had put on.

"Now, when you drop the rolling pin, all you have to do is pull up on the ropes until you can grab the pin," he said. "Of course, the better solution would be for you to just go home and take it easy for the next few weeks, but we all know how stubborn you are."

"We've been over this, Orson," Myra said. She toyed with the rope as she spoke. "I have three weeks to go until my due date. After that, I'm going to be at home with a new baby until I come back to work. I want to work until I can't any longer. I can't stand the thought of being home watching soap operas all day while I wait to not be pregnant anymore."

"That's actually really smart, Orson," Maggie said. She walked toward the baker's table and smiled.

"It reminds me of the eyeglass holders my grand-mother used to use to keep her glasses around her neck when she wasn't using them."

"That's where I got the idea," Orson said. "I remember seeing my grandma wearing them around her neck like that. As a little boy, I thought she looked ridiculous. Now, as an old man, I realize how right I was." He turned on his heel, snickering, and walked right back out of the kitchen.

Myra glanced at Maggie and then at Ruby. For a moment Maggie was scared she was going to burst out in tears. Instead, her face screwed up for a moment and then she burst out laughing. In less than a minute, the entire kitchen was filled with giggling donut makers.

Maggie wiped the tears flowing down her cheeks and shook her head. She struggled to form words between the giggles. "He's right, it does look ridiculous, but it works!"

Myra laughed even harder after Maggie spoke. "Oh," she said suddenly. "I think I just had a contraction!"

"Oh, no," Ruby said. Her face suddenly paled. "Maybe we should watch the giggle fits."

"At least you know what to do when you are

overdue and miserable waiting on the baby to come," Maggie said.

"What? Let Orson tie me to a rolling pin?" Myra asked. Her face was still red from laughing.

Maggie shook her head. "No, but you could let him talk. Let him go into a total stream of consciousness. He'll have you in labor before he even realizes how funny he is," she said. She waited until the laughter died down a bit to speak to the rest of them. She'd made sure Orson was covering the front and had called Naomi and Josie to the back.

"Ladies, I need to tell you all something," Maggie said. "Orson has the front for a second while we talk."

"What's this all about?" Ruby asked her. Maggie dropped her head for a moment. She should have informed Ruby prior to gathering everyone together. "I wanted to wait until all of you were here today to bring this up, although I should have let you know beforehand, Ruby. I'm sorry about that."

"Don't worry about it," she said. "What is going on?"

"Yesterday, when Ruby and I stopped in at the Hunter Springs location, Sheriff Mission pulled me aside and told me to be careful," Maggie said. "I should say, he told me to be extra careful."

"Any reason why?" Myra asked. Her eyebrows

knit together, and she frowned. "I have to use the restroom."

"Which requires a lot of effort right now, doesn't it?" Naomi asked. She stepped behind Myra and offered her an arm while she slid off the stool yet again.

"I'll make it quick. You should be in the bathroom by the time I finish," Maggie said.

"Deal," Myra said. "What's up?"

"Apparently, there have been reports of women being followed in our area. Brett said there isn't a reliable description of a suspect or a suspect's vehicle, but there have been several reports," Maggie said.

"Did he say where exactly this was happening?" Ruby asked.

"All over the county," Maggie said. "He told me there were five this week alone. As far as locations, he said it was mostly in isolated areas or rural settings. One woman was leaving a bar late at night and another one had pulled over on a rural road when she thought she had a flat tire."

"I wonder if Brooks knows about this yet?" Myra asked. She had stopped to catch her breath a few feet from the employee restroom. "He hasn't said anything."

"It could be that he hasn't had the chance to yet,"

Maggie said. "I think Brett just happened to be in Hunter Springs when we got there yesterday."

"Well, whatever you do, don't tell Orson about it. He's likely not to let me out of his sight. Not ever," Myra said before she closed the bathroom door.

CHAPTER THREE

Maggie pulled the door shut behind her and headed to her car. It was just after four in the afternoon, and she was headed for home, but only for a moment. She was going to shower and change and then head to Bradley's. Before she knew it, she was ready and on her way to her son's.

She walked in, her heart swelling with love. Wyatt was roaming around the house with a blanket trailing behind him, and Bradley knelt close by. As soon as Wyatt spotted her, he tossed his arms over his head and began to dance in place in delight.

Maggie swept into the room and scooped the baby up with a flourish. "How is my baby boy?" she asked and kissed his head.

"Just fine. Thanks for asking," Bradley said from above her.

"Ha, very funny," Maggie said. She held Wyatt aloft and grinned while her son cackled.

"Mimi," he said when she held him close to her chest. He cuddled against her and turned his head to deliver a wet, sloppy baby kiss right on her cheek.

"That never gets old," Maggie said. She handed Wyatt to his father and followed the pair into the well lit kitchen.

Maggie noticed her son had his laptop set up on the table. She took out hers from her laptop bag and settled into a chair, waiting for Bradley to join her.

"I wanted to go over a few things with you." Bradley handed the baby a sippy cup and a bowl of snacks. He scampered off to play while his father took a seat at the table. "I have the daily receipts you showed me how to print from the iPad at the donut shop," he said.

"Those totals should be automatically added to the bookkeeping program," Maggie said.

"They are." Bradley nodded. "It's not the daily totals I have an issue with, it's the vendor bills."

"Okay," Maggie said. She called up the program on her own computer and opened the credit section. She turned her screen to show him as she spoke.

"When you receive a bill, you add it here. There is a place for the invoice number and a description of the bill."

"Alright," Bradley said. "How do I set up a recurring charge?"

"You can do that," Maggie said, and showed him the process. "But you're still going to need to add the individual invoice number and date for the records."

Bradley nodded his head and added a few more notes. "My other question was, how do I print something that shows me the year-to-date or monthly earnings so far?"

Maggie shook her head. "Are you telling me that my Navy technology expert can't figure out this simple program?" she teased him.

"This Navy tech expert could build a security system for it, but just how to run the various features still escapes me," Bradley admitted.

"I think you're too smart for it and the program is too basic," Maggie said. "You're trying to make it more complicated than it is."

"You're probably right," he said. He watched as his mother made several clicks with the mouse. A second later, the printer in the extra bedroom he'd been using as a home office began to run.

"Okay," Bradley said. "I think I've got it."

"Good," Maggie said. "Now you do it."

"But you just did it. And now I have the report," Bradley argued.

"And then what happens the next time you want to run the report and I'm not here?" Maggie asked him.

Bradley grinned at his mother. "I call you up and you come and help me again?"

Maggie rolled her eyes. "Big Navy guy wants to call his mommy instead of trying to figure it out for himself."

"Fine," Bradley said. "Show me again." Bradley followed her steps and smiled when the printer fired up again.

"Good job." Maggie beamed. "Good boy!"

"Thank you," Wyatt said from his pile of toys. Maggie laughed until the tears filled her eyes.

"Now that we're finished with this, I wanted to share a new recipe with you," Bradley said.

"A new donut recipe?" Maggie asked.

Bradley nodded. "I think this will be a huge hit."

"I'm intrigued, but do you want to make them here or at the shop?"

"Let's go down to the old filling station," Bradley suggested. Despite the remodeling that had been done in the old building, the donut shop crew and the public alike still referred to it as "the old filling station."

"I'll follow you down there," Maggie said. "That way, I can simply head back home from the donut shop instead of coming all the way back to your house."

"Because it is so far to go," Bradley teased.

"You're becoming a regular comedian, aren't you?" Maggie tossed a kitchen towel at her son and headed for the door.

She drove the short distance to the filling station and waited for Bradley to arrive and unpack the baby from his car seat. He unlocked the door and flipped on the lights. Once he had the rest of the lights burning in the back, he returned to the front and turned off the lobby lights.

"Don't lecture me about the money-saving light-bulbs you ordered for me," he told his mother. "I shut those front lights off because there will be droves of people showing up and waiting for donuts, if I don't."

"You're kidding," Maggie said. "Even this late in the evening?"

"Definitely this late in the evening," Bradley said. He set the baby down in the corner play area he had created for him.

"Okay, so tell me about this mysterious new donut," Maggie said.

"Give me a second," Bradley said. He opened the cooler door and disappeared inside for a moment. When he returned, he had three large, light brown donuts on a plate. He placed the plate in the microwave oven and warmed the donuts for about ten seconds. "The fresh variety is better, of course, but this will give you a good idea."

When he pulled the microwave door open again, the kitchen filled with the aroma of a campfire breakfast.

"What am I smelling?" Maggie asked him.

"Just wait," Bradley said. "And for Pete's sake, be patient, Mother!"

Maggie waited while he set a donut on a separate plate for her. She took the fork he offered her and cut off a small piece of the donut. "What is this?" she asked, poking the fork into the side of the donut.

"Eat," he ordered.

Maggie picked up the piece she had cut off and placed it slowly into her mouth. She wasn't sure what to expect, but she found her mouth filled with the taste of a homemade breakfast. "Bacon? And pancakes?"

"Maple bacon," Bradley said. "I made a batch of

them and handed them out as samples. The crowd's response was almost like a frenzy. What do you think?" he asked her.

"Oh, that's a dangerous taste," she said, and picked up the donut with her hand. She took a larger bite out of it and closed her eyes. "That's very, very good."

"It's surprising that it's so good, right?" Bradley took a bite out of his own donut.

"Bite, Daddy," Wyatt said from his play area. "Bite."

Bradley tore a small piece from the third donut and handed it over.

"I want to make a batch tonight," Bradley said. "And you can take some home and have the rest of the staff try them out. Let me know what they think of them."

"Let's get started," Maggie said. She watched as Bradley gathered the ingredients for the donuts.

"I'm going to use the oven for the bacon," he said. He pulled out several metal baking sheets and carefully laid strips of bacon on each. He turned the oven on and waited for it to preheat. The still new smell of the oven filled the kitchen.

Maggie helped by mixing the flour, baking powder, baking soda, salt, and sugar together in a large bowl. She added eggs, vegetable oil, butter, and milk to the large stand mixer and turned it on to mix. Carefully, she measured the vanilla and maple flavorings and added them while Bradley added the dry ingredients.

The batter rested while the bacon cooled and then Bradley pulled the strips from each pan and pressed them between two pieces of paper towels. "I learned the hard way to remove as much excess grease as possible," he explained. He then placed each slice together on a cutting board and cut the bacon up into small pieces.

When the bacon was cut small enough, he turned the mixer on low and added some of the bacon to the batter.

"Wait, you are only adding some of the bacon?" Maggie pointed out. "What are you going to do with the rest of it?"

"I think I'll add it to the top with the maple flavored icing this time," Bradley said. "Wait until you taste a fresh one."

Maggie waited while her son added the batter to the automatic donut machine. He mixed up powdered sugar, maple flavoring, water, and real maple syrup into a thick glaze. He then removed the finished donuts from the machine and set them on the table.

One at a time, he dipped the donuts into the bowl of icing and then dipped the iced donuts into the bacon pieces.

"Wow, these are pretty labor-intensive," Maggie said.

"They are, which is why I plan to offer them on a limited basis and charge more per dozen than normal," he said. "I'm going to make large quantities available by pre-ordering only."

"That's a pretty good idea," Maggie said. "But the danger is in how they make the entire place smell. I can't wait to try another one!"

Bradley handed a warm donut to her on a napkin and waited for her to sample it. "Well? What do you think?" he asked.

Maggie bit into the fresh donut and immediately took a second bite. "Oh, that is even better warm," she said. "I can't wait for these to show up in my display case. And boy, am I glad we made the choice to open a new place. Just think, this could have been a doll shop. Instead, it employs my son... the man who made the best donut I've ever tasted in my life. Seriously, Bradley, these are amazing."

CHAPTER FOUR

Maggie carried two large donut boxes outside. She placed them in her car and headed back inside the donut shop to hug her grandson once more before she left for home.

"Don't forget, I want to know what everyone's reaction is to the donuts," Bradley said when she hugged him as well.

"Send over the recipe to me as soon as you can, please," Maggie said. "By the way, where did you find the recipe? I'm shocked that it worked in the donut machine."

"I tweaked a random recipe I found online until it worked as I wanted it to," Bradley said. "At first, the bacon burned while the donuts fried. That's when I started baking the bacon."

"Look at you being all brilliant and entrepreneurial," Maggie said and pinched his cheek.

"Jeez, Mom," he said and blushed slightly. "I am an adult, you know."

"And a very special one at that," she teased him. He rolled his eyes at her and pushed her out the door to her car.

Maggie headed out of town toward the highway. She was distracted by the heavy maple and bacon aroma in her car. She laughed when she imagined how Brett or Brooks would respond to the news of a donut with bacon in it.

She glanced at the time on her radio display. It was a little past eight. The moon shone overhead, and she was almost entirely alone on the road. A few cars passed her from the opposite direction, but only one or two cars had passed her from behind.

She was suddenly aware of a small SUV behind her. The vehicle had come close to her and then backed off. The smile left her face and her nerves stood on end. Brett's words of warning filled her mind at that moment.

She reached a part of the highway that stretched to four lanes. She moved to the right lane and slowed her car down to five miles below the speed limit. The SUV drew closer, and Maggie waited for it to pass her by. She told herself that the vehicle would move around her. She could speed up and get on home after it passed.

But the SUV slowed down as well and moved into the right lane behind her. Her heart beat faster in her chest. She sped up and moved into the left lane. The vehicle switched lanes behind her and pulled up close enough that she could decipher the color, make, and model.

The highway narrowed again as they passed through a rural area. Maggie gripped the steering wheel as tight as she could. She sped up again, this time going as fast as ten miles over the speed limit. The SUV kept pace with her. She began to shake as she drove. Her body shivered from fear and anxiety. This felt all too real after what had happened with her, Ruby, and Naomi not that long ago.

"Think, think," she said out loud. She began to count backward from ten, hoping to force her mind to snap out of the fear and into thinking mode.

"Seven, six, five, four," she said, then stopped. She pushed the phone button on her steering wheel and instructed the computer to dial Brett on his cell phone.

The line went straight to voicemail. She left a

description of where she was and the vehicle behind her. Thirty seconds later, her phone rang.

"What is he doing now?" Brett demanded in lieu of a hello.

"He's driving about a car's length back," she said.

"What can you see of the driver?" he asked her.

"Uh, not much," Maggie said. She slowed down a little and let the vehicle get closer. She glanced in the rearview mirror as long as she safely could and described what she could see. "Baseball cap pulled low. The cap looks blue."

"Tell me about the cap," Brett said. His voice was smooth and soothing. Maggie could hear the engine of his vehicle rev as he increased his speed.

"I see two letters, a logo of some sort on the front," she said. "Oh! It's a Royals cap! Kansas City Royals!"

"What about the driver himself?" Brett asked her. "Can you tell the skin color or height?"

"I think he's wearing sunglasses, which is weird at eight o'clock at night," she said. "The only thing I can tell is medium to light-colored skin."

"So, you think he has white, or maybe light brown skin?"

"Yes, uh-huh," she said. "And not very big. Sort

of skinny. Narrow shoulders. Average height. His head doesn't come above the head rest."

"That's good, Maggie," he said. "Very good. Now, I want you to tell me what you see around you. Have you made it to the Pilot station yet?"

Maggie tried to gauge her proximity to the place he mentioned. She could see a tall, neon sign ahead of her. "I'm maybe a mile away from it," she said.

"Okay," Brett said. "What I want you to do is slow down like you're going to get off there. Move into the off ramp and see if he follows you. At the last second, if you safely can, yank the wheel back to the left and head for the Dogwood Mountain exit. I have a deputy about three minutes out from the truck stop. I'm on the other side of the county, but Brooks is going to meet you just inside the city limits."

Maggie waited until the off ramp was in view and then slowed her car down slightly. She veered right and slowed down more, but didn't turn on her signal. The SUV slowed down and followed her over. She counted to five, and then yanked her wheel to the left and headed back down on the highway.

She watched for the other vehicle to follow suit in her rearview mirror. Thankfully, the vehicle seemed to continue on to the Pilot station. The exit for

Dogwood Mountain appeared a short time later, and she felt her heart slow to its normal pace.

"You okay?" Brooks asked her when she rolled down her window. "Brett was almost sick that he wasn't close enough to help."

"I'm okay," she said. "I just hope the deputies got to him, whoever he was."

"I haven't heard anything one way or the other just yet, but I will let you know if I do," Brooks said. "For now, I'm going to follow you home and walk through the house before you go inside."

"Brooks, you really don't have to do that," Maggie said. She was suddenly embarrassed by the fuss he was making over her.

"Yes, I do, actually," he said with a smile. "For one, Brett told me to do it and I am not about to go against his orders, official or not. And two, I would be livid if it was my wife and he didn't do the same thing for her."

Maggie smiled and waited while he returned to his car. She thought to point out to him the difference in his analogy. She was nowhere close to being Brett's wife, and his wife was young and quite pregnant. But she decided to let the point go when she pulled into her driveway. Brooks approached her car window again. She handed over her keys and waited while he made his way through her house. She stepped out of her car and picked up the donut boxes from the passenger seat.

"Here," she said, handing him one when he returned. "For your trouble. Just let me know what you think and the reactions of anyone else who tries them."

"What are they?" he asked her. "Are they something different from normal?"

Maggie smiled. "Bradley made them," she said. "They are maple bacon donuts."

Brooks opened the box and inhaled deeply. "Oh, these are dangerous," he said. "And the box feels warm still."

"That's what I told him," Maggie said. She walked toward her back door. "I just wish they were the only dangerous things around."

CHAPTER FIVE

Just after three the following morning, Maggie gave up on trying to get sleep. She threw the covers back and sat up. She dressed quickly and turned the alarm off on her phone. Her head ached from the lack of sleep. When she was able to sleep, she had dreams of dark-colored SUVs following her home.

Before she left for the donut shop, Maggie fixed a cup of coffee from her single-serve coffee maker and poured it into a travel mug from her kitchen cabinet. She was quite sure she'd need as much caffeine as she could handle for the day ahead.

She headed out the door with the box of donuts under her arm. When she pulled up in the alley behind her shop a moment later, she carried the donuts inside and flipped on all the lights from the front of the building to the back. She set the donuts on the baker's table and walked through every inch of the building before she peered outside through the front windows. She found no sign of a SUV in the parking lot, dark-colored or otherwise.

Maggie sighed when she returned to the kitchen area. She hugged her arms around her middle and suddenly regretted showing up so early for work. She yawned and headed back up front to start a pot of coffee. She hit the switch on the coffee maker as lights shone through the front windows and lit up the dining room. Her heart froze in her chest for a split second, but her fears were calmed when the driver of the car shut their lights off and stepped out of the vehicle. Maggie smiled when she recognized Brett. She headed for the door and unlocked it to let him in.

"What are you doing here?" she asked. "I didn't expect to see you."

"I was hoping to catch you at home before you left for work," he said. "But when your car wasn't there, I thought I'd try here."

Maggie let him in and locked the door behind him. "I'm surprised you didn't park in the back," she said.

"I saw you through the windows up front," he

said. "I have some news for you about what happened last night."

"And I have something for you to try in the back," Maggie said. She wasn't specifically trying to avoid the subject of the car following her last night; she just needed a breath before he launched into whatever he came to tell her.

"Oh, I'm intrigued," Brett said, and followed her through the swinging door into the kitchen. "What could you have for me to try?" He wiggled his eyebrows and leaned in close.

"Stop." Maggie laughed and pushed his shoulder back. "Bradley made a new recipe, a maple bacon donut."

"You're kidding," Brett said. "What do I have to do to get one of those?"

Maggie said nothing but headed to get one of the donuts. She pulled it out of the donut box and set it on a plate to warm in the microwave for a short time. Instantly, the entire kitchen smelled like bacon and maple syrup. "Let me know what you think," she said. "I'm seriously considering adding this to the menu here."

Brett picked up the donut and took a huge bite. His eyes widened and his mouth spread into a grin around the donut. "Oh," he said slowly when he was finished. "That's too good."

"I take it you approve?" Maggie asked him.

"I almost think this has to be illegal," he said. "At least, it feels like it should be."

"Well, that settles it," Maggie said. "These are going on the menu."

"I didn't know I had that kind of sway with you," Brett teased. He finished off the donut before he spoke again. "Anyway, I wanted to stop by and tell you what happened with the traffic stop last night after the vehicle behind you pulled into the Pilot station."

"Okay," Maggie said. She decided to sit down on a stool while he spoke.

"A couple of deputies found him right away based on your description. He was wearing sunglasses, like you said," Brett continued. "But I don't think he was following you. Not deliberately anyway."

"You don't think so? What about the way he slowed down and then hurried up behind me?"

"Deputies took him into custody and held him at the sheriff's office for a little while for questioning," Brett said. "I guess I should start saying that they held him at my office. That still takes some getting used to."

"What did they find out?" Maggie asked.

"Honestly, I spoke with him as well and I think it was just a simple misunderstanding," Brett admitted. "I know that might sound crazy to you, but he was just trying to get to the gas station."

"Why was he wearing sunglasses, then?" Maggie asked.

"He had lost his eyeglasses, and he is very light sensitive," Brett said. "He shouldn't have been driving and he won't be driving again any time soon, but I don't think he was stalking you. And we are quite sure that he isn't our guy."

"So, this was all just a misunderstanding, as you said a moment ago," Maggie said, still not quite sure.

Brett shook his head. "Not that your instincts weren't right on target after what I shared with you the other day," he said. "He said he drove close to the car in front of him in the hopes he could see the exit better, but then he worried he was getting too close and tailgating the car."

"Do you believe his story, Brett? I mean, are you completely sure that he told you the truth last night?"

Brett nodded. "His daughter picked him up and confirmed everything he told us," he said. "She promised that his car would be retrieved from the gas station, and he would not drive again until he sees his eye doctor."

"Alright, then," Maggie said. "That makes me feel a lot better." She slipped off of her stool and headed back out front. "Why don't we sit for a minute and enjoy a cup of coffee? I think I'd like to start the day at work with a coffee break and a deep breath."

CHAPTER SIX

Myra had arrived at the donut shop around the same time as always, and Naomi was due in shortly afterward. Ruby made small talk while she set to work putting together the lunch boxes at the prep table. She was switching the menu around to reflect more of the fall season.

"Why does it smell like pancakes and bacon in here?" Naomi asked when she arrived.

"I didn't want to bring it up, but do you have any more of them here?" Myra asked. She was inside the cooler with the door open, gathering ingredients for the cinnamon rolls.

"Any more what?" Ruby asked.

"What's everyone talking about?" Naomi asked. She pulled her apron off the hook outside of the store room and ventured inside the cooler with Myra. "What on earth do you have in that box?"

Maggie left her station between the automatic donut machines and headed to the cooler. Ruby set down her basket of apples for the apple slaw and followed her.

Myra stood in the middle of the cooler with her hand in the donut box Maggie had brought with her from Hunter Springs. Her cheeks were filled out with the remnants of one donut, and she had her hand on a second. "I thought I went to heaven for a minute. I couldn't resist," she said around a mouth full of food. "Sorry, Maggie. It's the baby's fault."

"How pathetic, blaming an unborn child," Ruby said with mock seriousness. She removed the box from Myra's eager hands and opened it up fully. "What in the heck is this?"

"Bradley tried a new recipe last night and sent some with me for everyone to try," she said.

"How did Myra know about them before now?" Naomi asked. She reached her hand in for a donut.

"Because I had what I thought was a run-in with a bad guy last night on the highway on my way home from Hunter Springs," Maggie said. "And Brett arranged for Brooks to meet me inside the city limits and escort me home. So, he got one box."

"Someone followed you?" Ruby asked suddenly. The maple bacon donuts were forgotten for a moment. "Are you okay?"

Maggie nodded her head and moved out of the cooler and back into the kitchen. "Brett had his deputies meet the man at the truck stop out on the highway before the Dogwood Mountain exit," she explained. "It turns out that he was just an old man with bad eyesight who had no business driving at all, let alone at night without the right eyeglasses."

"It's so strange how they haven't come up with a decent suspect description or at least an idea of what the vehicle looks like," Naomi said.

"The police are trying," Myra said. She moved slowly back out of the cooler to the baker's table and resumed her seat. Her face was no longer bright and smiling.

"Oh, Myra. I didn't mean that as a dig against law enforcement," Naomi said. "I was speaking about the lack of witnesses coming forward."

"No offense taken," Myra said. "I'm just worried right now."

"What's the matter, Myra?" Ruby moved suddenly to her side. "Are you feeling alright?"

"Yeah, is everything okay?" Maggie added.

"Yeah, I'm fine," Myra said. "The problem is that I want a third one of those donuts."

"When are we going to start making them?" Ruby asked. She popped a piece into her mouth and closed her eyes.

"They're even better warm," Myra whispered.

"We can make a batch this morning and hand them out as samples to gauge interest," Maggie suggested. "Bradley gave me the recipe and showed me a few shortcuts for making them."

"And the teacher becomes the student," Ruby said.

Maggie rewarded her comment by tossing a clean apron at her head. "You're proud of the kid and you know it," she said.

"You bet I am! And I'm proud of you for being willing to learn from him," Ruby replied.

Maggie gathered the dry ingredients from the store room and instructed Naomi on making the bacon in the oven and explained why. She mixed the batter into the large stand mixer and then stirred in the bacon once it was cooled. Naomi manned the donut machine while Maggie mixed the icing.

After the maple bacon donuts were made, Maggie began mixing the batter for the apple cider donuts she planned to accompany Ruby's apple slaw in the boxed lunches. Orson arrived shortly after opening and headed straight for the kitchen.

"You are creating quite the buzz out there," he said and headed for the warming rack where the bacon donuts were cooling on trays. He picked up a napkin and carefully removed one of the fresh donuts, and headed back out front.

"Wait, Orson!" Maggie followed him out to the dining room. "What do you mean, we have created a buzz out here?" She whispered her question to him. Orson ignored her and headed for the Old Timer's table with his maple bacon donut. Now she knew there was no actual buzz. Orson had just set her up for it to happen.

"Hey, what is that?" Delbert, one of the old men who sat at the table daily, demanded to know.

"Ask her," Orson said. He pointed right at Maggie and took a huge bite out of the donut in the napkin.

"Well?" Delbert asked. "Why aren't those in the display case, or better yet, why aren't they sitting in front of me right now?"

"It's a new recipe and we will have samples available soon," Maggie said. She shot Orson a warning look. He replied with a cheesy grin and a mouth filled with donut.

"I'd better get one," Delbert said.

Maggie sighed and clasped her hands in front of her chest. "Delbert, I will rush right back to the kitchen and bring out another donut for you before I do anything else," she said. "Okay?"

"Can you bring me another one?" Orson asked. He offered her another cheesy grin.

"You, sir, are pushing it," Maggie said. She tried to appear severe, but only shook her head and laughed instead.

"Orson is shoving me right under the bus, left and right," she said to the other women when she headed back to the kitchen. She grabbed a tray of maple bacon donuts and headed toward the door.

"Where are you going with those?" Ruby asked.

"Out there," Maggie said. "Thanks to Orson, everyone knows about them, and everybody wants one."

"I'm going to start a second batch once Myra is finished with the chocolate glazed donuts," Naomi announced.

Maggie nodded her head. "You might as well," she said. "So much for testing out the recipe and serving them every once in a while."

When she pushed herself through the swinging door again, she headed straight for the Old Timer's table and handed a fresh donut to Delbert.

"Thank you, sweets," Delbert said.

"Where's mine?" Orson asked her.

"Orson Hawley," she said and shook her head, and then set a fresh donut on the napkin in front of him.

"Thank you, ma'am," Orson said and grinned again.

Maggie shook her head and rolled her eyes. She headed for the display case and set the tray on the top, then looked up to see a crowd forming. She spent the next several moments handing out the donut samples to her eager customers. She announced that the next round would be priced accordingly and made a mental note to add a sign to the menu board. Larger quantities would require at least a day's notice.

The tray was quickly emptied. Maggie turned to head back to the kitchen with the empty tray, but she waited when a disheveled, desperate woman rushed inside the doors and headed for the counter.

"I'm looking for Maggie Sharpe," she said.

Maggie stepped backward and was stunned slightly for a moment. She studied the woman before she answered. Her dark hair stuck out in all directions from the loose ponytail tied on the top of her head. She stood about the same height as Maggie and was close to the same weight and age.

"Can I help you?" Maggie asked her. She pushed the tray under the counter and rested her hands on the counter.

"Oh, are you Maggie?"

Maggie shot Orson a look. The old man was already turned toward her and watching the exchange. She nodded and repeated the offer to help her. "What can I do for you?"

The woman rushed forward and clasped Maggie's hands in her own. "Oh, I wanted to stop by and check on you as fast as I could."

"Check on me? Why would you need to check on me?" Maggie asked. She carefully removed her hands from the woman's grasp.

"Oh, I'm so sorry," the woman said. She lowered her voice. "I should explain to you who I am."

"That would be a good start," Maggie agreed.

"Okay, my name is Erin Johnson," she said. "I heard about the incident last night on the highway with the stalker."

Maggie stepped back another step and eyed the woman carefully. "Whoa," Maggie said. "How on earth did you hear about that?"

"Oh, I'm sorry," Erin said. "You were the latest victim of the stalker. I heard your name over the police scanner and looked you up and found out where you work."

"You figured out who I was based on my name being read over the police scanner?"

Erin nodded her head. "I had to come and see you and find out if you were alright," she said. "What can you recall about the man in the SUV? Did you get a good look at him?"

"I don't know what you heard, Erin, but I was not a victim of a stalker last night," she said. She lowered her voice and hoped the woman on the other side of the counter would follow suit. "It was a misunderstanding."

"But he was following you," Erin said. Her face was almost childlike in its eagerness. "You were the latest victim."

"I'm sorry," Maggie said. "But that's not what happened. The sheriff himself interviewed the driver. He was not stalking me."

"No, you're wrong," Erin said. She moved her hands from the counter and frowned. "I heard it myself. I had to come and see you to find out if you were okay."

"Like I said, it was not what you think," Maggie said. She was beginning to fear some sort of a scene right there in her donut shop. "Why are you so interested in this, anyway?"

"Because." Erin stepped back to the counter and narrowed her eyes. "I'm the one who has been calling in about him. I have tried for a week to get the sheriff to listen to me about this man. And when I heard that there was another victim, I knew I wasn't crazy."

CHAPTER SEVEN

"I don't think she heard a single word I said." Maggie stood in the middle of the kitchen, flanked on one side with Orson retelling the interaction to Ruby, who was taking in every last word.

"I think you ought to tell Brett about what happened here," Ruby said. "I'm worried about this woman."

"Why are you worried?" Naomi asked from the sink. She had shooed Myra away from washing the dishes and insisted on her remaining on a stool and off of her feet.

"She seems off," Ruby said. "I don't know if she's desperately hoping someone verifies her delusion for her or if there really is a stalker out there. And if it's the latter, she needs to give the police more information."

"I don't know," Naomi said. "I mean, I've known some women who were the victims of a stalker, and it is really hard to believe sometimes. People can be really scary."

Ruby smiled. "I understand that. I really do," she said. "But I'm worried about this woman's actions in particular. She didn't seem to want to take Maggie's word for it. That opens up an entirely new set of possibilities."

"I just don't want to demonize someone that might be a victim in any case," Naomi said.

"Demonize? That's a pretty strong word," Ruby said.

"It's hard to demonize someone who might be a little wacky in the first place," Orson mumbled. "You didn't see her or hear her. She was not hearing one word Maggie said."

"I just don't know that we need to report it to the sheriff is all," Naomi said. "It might make more trouble for her than she needs."

"But it is important to the overall case," Myra piped up. "Several calls have already come in reporting a stalker and as far as I understand, no one has left a name so far. They have just reported things anonymously. And besides, I texted Brooks about it. The sheriff knows."

"I understand," Naomi said. "I only want to make sure people are kept safe. But that includes you guys, too."

"Yeah, and that's just the way things go around here, Naomi," Myra said. "I'm really not trying to make you upset or anything, but that's the way we do things. We stay in close contact with the police and would even if we weren't in relationships with them."

Naomi nodded her head. "I guess I just have a different sort of relationship with law enforcement." She dried her hands on a towel and walked out of the kitchen.

"I really didn't mean to offend her," Myra whispered.

"Don't worry about it," Ruby said. She hugged Myra from behind and offered her a water bottle. "Naomi has lived a life we have never dealt with."

Maggie opened her mouth to chime in but was cut off by her phone ringing. She moved quickly to her office to take the call. "Tell me about this woman who stopped by," Brett said on the other end of the phone. "The way Myra explained it to Brooks, she acted a little strange."

"She just wouldn't hear me when I tried to tell her

that I wasn't being followed last night after all," Maggie said.

"Did she give you the impression that she was under the influence at all, or maybe not in her right mind?" Brett asked.

"I don't think I'm qualified to make that statement, but something was definitely off," Maggie replied. "That's for sure."

"I understand your point," he said. "I just want to know whether or not the person making these claims is on the up and up. There are too many odd things about this to not consider it."

"I don't understand," Maggie said. "It's true that no one at all from the police has talked to her in person yet?"

"It's true. We haven't," he told her. "The person who called in these reports claimed to be scared and didn't want to give her name. She just gave a vague description of the situation."

"And how many calls were made in total?" she asked him. "Have there been more?"

"Just the five, same as before."

"And you're thinking they are all from the same woman?"

"No, actually," Brett said. "We think it was at least two different women. Unless the caller is some kind of a gifted voice actor, I heard at least two different voices."

"If she came out to see me, I wonder why she doesn't just come forward to the police?" Maggie said. "There's nothing I can do that you guys can't."

"She might be scared out of her mind," Brett said. "Do me a favor? If she comes back to the donut shop, will you encourage her to talk to me?"

"I'll do my best," Maggie said. She ended the call and placed her phone back on her desk.

Naomi was waiting outside of the office when she emerged from it. "Hey, can we talk for a moment?"

"Sure," Maggie said. She stepped back into her office. "What's up?"

"I just wanted to apologize for the way I sounded a little while ago," Naomi said. "It's just that in my past life, well, let's just say that I have been a frightened woman before. And there is not a whole lot about it that is cut and dry."

"I had a feeling your response was based on some personal experience," Maggie said. "I don't think you have anything to apologize for."

"That's kind of you," Naomi said. "I appreciate it."

"No, it isn't necessarily that," Maggie said. "It's just the truth. I'm having a hard time understanding why this woman even came in to the donut shop to speak with me in the first place. But I don't have any difficulty understanding why you might be defensive of someone in her case."

Naomi thanked her again and left the office to head back out front. Maggie busied herself changing the upcoming food vendor orders to ensure she had enough to cover the demand for the new donut flavor.

"It's amazing how expensive bacon can be," she told Ruby when she walked back into the kitchen.

"I wonder if the grocery store might offer us a better price?" Ruby asked. "Sometimes going with a local provider can significantly cut costs."

"Maybe I'll head over there and find out," Maggie said.

"At the very least, you might be able to get the information to order directly, instead of going through our normal supplier," Ruby suggested. "Check on the maple syrup, too."

"Good idea," Maggie said. She pulled her purse out from behind her office chair and headed out the door.

CHAPTER EIGHT

Maggie parked her car close to the entrance of the grocery store. For the middle of the day, the parking lot was rather empty, but she wasn't complaining. She wanted to speak with the manager about ordering bacon and possibly pure maple syrup as well, and doing so when it was slower was a better idea for them both.

She headed into the store and grabbed a cart, mainly out of habit, and walked to the breakfast aisle to price the syrup. Even at retail price, the syrup was less than she could find from her suppliers. She grabbed four bottles and headed toward the meat department in the deli, where she was sure to run into the manager she most wanted to speak with.

"Hi, Allen," she called to the butcher behind the

meat counter. "Is your manager back there?" Allen rushed off to the back and came out, telling her he'd be right with her. While she waited for the manager to come to her, Maggie decided she would purchase a couple of thick and tender beef filets for dinner.

The manager appeared from the back. "I'm Ralph. How can I help you?" He was dressed in a white shirt and tie and, with his well-combed silver hair and black glasses, reminded her of a grocery store manager from a bygone era. In fact, she searched her memory for the 1980s sitcom character he most resembled.

"Hi, Ralph," she said. "I'm Maggie. I don't know if you remember me, but I own the donut shop here in town."

"And the new one in Hunter Springs as well, if I am not mistaken," Ralph said with a smile. "What can I do for you?"

"Oh, have you been to the new location?" she asked.

Ralph nodded and smiled. "Yes, I live in Hunter Springs. Your donut shop has now become my daily early morning stop," he said. "I like the crew and I especially love the new bacon-flavored donuts. Pair that with a cup of that strong, black coffee and I feel like a man in his prime again."

Maggie chuckled out loud. "Well, thank you on both parts," she said. "The main guy over there, tall and blonde? That's my son, Bradley. The maple bacon donuts were actually his creation. And we are going to offer them here at this location as well."

"Oh, my," Ralph said. Even his eyes smiled at the news. "I'm ecstatic about that! But I'm sure that isn't the reason you came to see me."

"No, it isn't, actually," Maggie said. "I've checked with my own vendors and suppliers and have found that the bacon we want for the donuts and the pure maple syrup is a lot more expensive there than simply stopping by here to purchase them."

"But hoping you will find the right amount to run two businesses is not sustainable," he said. "I can get you a price break on the maple syrup. That won't be a problem, with a minimum order, of course. The bacon is a different story, given the constant fluctuations in meat prices."

"That's a fact," Maggie said. "Right now, we're using real bacon to make these donuts, and I'd like to keep it that way. But nobody wants to pay five bucks for a single donut."

Ralph smiled again. "Right," he said. "What I can do is put you in touch with a local farmer who likes to sell his bacon at local markets. He has approached me, but I can't accommodate him, of course, being a part of a chain of stores and all."

"Locally sourced bacon sounds really good in an advertisement," Maggie said.

"Exactly," Ralph said. He excused himself to his office and returned with an order slip for the syrup and the number of the farmer he spoke of. "Just give this guy a call and tell him what you need. If he doesn't have the capacity for your donut shops, just give me a call back and I'll order the bacon for you. You might not save a ton of money, but it's better than nothing."

"Any saving is worth it," Maggie added. She thanked him again and headed for the cashier with her purchases.

When she left the store and headed for the parking lot, she was surprised to see a dozen more cars in the lot than when she had arrived less than twenty minutes prior. Maggie pulled out her phone and fired off a text to Brett to meet her at her house for dinner. She turned on her phone's camera, ready to snap a shot of the steaks as she put them in the car.

"I would accuse you of working hard, but I can see that you are hardly working," a semi-familiar voice called to her from a few parking spaces down.

Maggie looked up to see Preston Nance approach.

Since taking over the bookstore, he had turned it into some sort of hybrid business. Just what his business was, she still wasn't sure. He dabbled in real estate and had purchased several run-down rentals across town, including the place Naomi lived outside of Dogwood Mountain.

Above all else, he tended to be an unfriendly, cold sort of man. Preston raised a set of keys and clicked the lock button and waited for the car to respond with the appropriate chirp, indicating that it was locked.

Maggie was not surprised to see the car that responded was a large, luxury sports car, in dark blue, of course. She figured a man like him would drive something big and comfortable, but with the motor capacity that would roar down the highway. And the dark blue simply matched every outfit she had ever seen him wear, always in either black or navy blue.

"As a matter of fact, I'm here after some ingredients," Maggie said in her own defense. "Not that it's any of your business."

"Whoa, she has a tongue that responds in kind," he said. He smiled for the first time since she'd met him. "Have I hit a nerve?"

"What do you want, Mr. Nance?"

"Oh, I was just wondering how a fellow business owner is able to step away from her work and enjoy a grocery shopping trip in the middle of the day," he replied. "How very mid-century modern housewife of you!"

"How very ignorant of you, Mr. Nance," she said, ready to tell him he was also a business owner who was at the grocery store in the middle of the day. She could feel the anger welling up in her middle, and for once, she wasn't about to slink into a fit of shyness. And besides, Ruby was not around this time to answer him back for her. "If you had any idea how to run a successful food service establishment, you would know that an occasional trip to the grocery store is common. I can doubly reassure you that I know what I am doing. I do own two locations."

"Oh, expanded, did we?" He suddenly seemed quite pale. "Well, congratulations, Miss Sharpe. You have bested the local town snob. Good day." He clicked his heels and tipped his nonexistent hat in her direction and headed inside.

Maggie shook her head before she got into her car.

"Wait! Wait, Maggie," she heard another voice calling to her, only this one was female and quite shrill sounding.

"This was the wrong time to come to the grocery store," she said when she looked up and saw Erin

Johnson advancing toward her car. She pulled another doe-eyed woman along behind her.

"Who was that man?" she demanded. "What was he saying to you?"

"Who, Preston Nance? He's just a smart mouthed business owner who thinks he's above the rest of us locals," she said, a little shocked at her own summary of the man. "What are you doing here?"

"Well, my business partner, Lana, and I just stopped by here for some food and we saw that man harassing you in the parking lot," she said. Her hand moved to her throat in a dramatic expression. Maggie looked for a moment to see if there was a strand of pearls in her grasp.

"He wasn't harassing me," Maggie said. "Please stop putting words in my mouth. Now, if you will excuse me, I have a business to run. Have a good day."

She started her car and noticed the phone still in her hand, and still on the camera app. While she was putting it away, the phone snapped a photo. Maggie sighed. She'd planned on sending Brett a photo of the steaks, but she definitely wasn't going to send him a hideous selfie. She rushed to get herself settled in her car before anyone else interrupted her and then eased her car in reverse and drove out of the parking lot, eager to get back to work.

"Someone called in and reported another stalking," Brett told her when he arrived twenty minutes late for their dinner. "I was at my office for a few extra minutes trying to get all of the details I could."

"Did the caller leave a name this time?" Maggie asked him.

"Only a first name, which, given the ongoing nature of the investigation, you know I can't divulge," he said. "And that's assuming it was a real name."

Maggie knew that already, but her curiosity raged. She wondered if Erin had been the caller. And if she had, what was the woman's story? Was she a victim who saw perpetrators everywhere?

"What are you thinking about?" Brett asked her. He turned his steak on her small outdoor grill and sighed. "This was a wonderful surprise after the day I had, by the way."

"Wait until you try the red wine I have in the pantry," Maggie said. She stepped inside the kitchen and returned with two half-full glasses. "This should pair nicely with a filet as tender as these."

"Thank you," Brett said when she handed him a glass. "But you didn't answer my question," he said. "What's on your mind?"

Maggie sipped her wine and settled into her chair. Brett checked the steaks, then joined her. "At least it's a nice evening," she said. For fall, it was surprisingly warm. "And as for what's on my mind, I had another run-in with Erin while I was at the grocery store earlier today."

"Oh, yeah? How did that go?"

"You remember Preston Nance, the man who bought Faylene's old bookstore?"

Brett nodded. "I've met him. Pleasant sort of fellow," he said.

"Only, not at all," Maggie said, quirking a brow. "Anyway, he surprised me while I was getting into my car. We exchanged a few spitting words and then he left to go inside the store."

"Spitting words? You?"

"Don't seem so shocked," Maggie said. "But yes. I was actually a little on fire with the zingers today."

"Atta girl." Brett beamed.

"Anyway, when I turned to finish texting you, I set the bags in the car and turned around to hear a woman's voice calling out to ask me if I was okay," she said. "Turns out it was Erin and some wide-eyed thing along with her named Lana."

"What did she have to say?"

"She asked me in a very panicked voice who he was and if he was harassing me," Maggie said. "Both of them looked like they had just seen a huge dinosaur escape from a remote island or something."

"A Jurassic Park reference," Brett said. "I'm impressed."

"Anyway, I thought the entire exchange was weird." Maggie tipped her glass up and swallowed a long draw of wine.

"It sounds like your assessment is right," he said.

"What did the woman who called in say?" Maggie asked. "Was she accosted or anything?"

"No, just harassed on the road," he said. "She said she was able to see the man clearly."

"Is she going to come in and give a description, or did she already?"

"No." Brett shook his head and sighed. "We tried, but she isn't willing. I guess she is still too scared, or they are too scared."

"What about the vehicle? Was it similar to some of the others?"

Brett shrugged. "No, this one was a dark-colored

car," he said. "Why do I get the feeling you are cooking something up?"

Maggie shook her head and studied the wine in her glass. She swirled it around a few times before she answered. "I don't know what I'm thinking, to be honest with you, Brett," she said. "But I can tell you that something is off. Something about this whole matter doesn't add up to me."

"And you're going to look into it," Brett said. "Just be careful. Whatever you do, be careful, okay?"

"Always." Maggie smiled.

Brett placed both steaks onto plates while Maggie headed back to the kitchen for the roasted red potatoes she had left in the air fryer. "More wine?" she asked him when she returned.

"Of course," he said. "Although you do know that this means I won't be leaving for a little while."

"Why do you think I offered?" Maggie said with a wink.

CHAPTER NINE

It was well after eleven when Brett had left to return home the night before. Despite the late night, Maggie arose on time and headed in to work. For once, Ruby beat her there. She unlocked the back door and headed inside.

"Ruby," she called. "Are you in here?" She moved through the dark kitchen and pushed open the swinging door.

"Over here," Ruby said. She leaned against one of the windows, gazing outside into the parking lot.

"What are you doing?" Maggie asked. Ruby barely cast a glance in her direction. Her eyes were fixed on the dark parking lot. "Ruby?"

She jumped a little and turned her body to face

Maggie. "I'm sorry, I just had an interesting experi-ence on the drive here," she said.

Maggie studied her best friend. "What is going on? What happened?"

"I don't want you to get upset or anything, but I was followed here this morning," Ruby said.

"Followed," Maggie repeated, swallowing hard.

Ruby straightened the chairs by the window and bent down to pick up a loose napkin on the floor. "By a truck," she said. "They rushed up behind me and then backed off, back and forth all the way from the blacktop road and into the parking lot. And before you ask me, yes, I called Brett. And I gave him the only description I have. Once I got here, the truck raced in a circle around the parking lot and then took off."

"Oh, my gosh," Maggie said. She held her arms out and pulled her reluctant friend into a hug. "Are you alright?"

"Yeah, yeah," Ruby said dismissively. "I'm fine. I'm just frustrated. I knew about the stories of the alleged serial stalker. And when that lady came in here the other day, whatever her name was..."

"Erin Johnson," Maggie offered.

"Yeah, Erin," Ruby said. "But I didn't believe her. Not one word of what she said. I don't know what I thought about her reasons, but I know I didn't believe a word of what she had to say."

"And now?"

"Well, now I know what happened to me this morning and I know what I saw," Ruby said.

"I'm so sorry," Maggie said. "For what it's worth, I didn't believe much of what she had to say either. It's all weird. I can't put my finger on it, but it just seems off somehow."

"That might be, but I can tell you I didn't imagine the person following me," Ruby said.

"I believe you. I don't doubt you for a minute," Maggie said. "I just don't know what any of it means."

"Anyway, Brett will be here soon," Ruby said. "Brooks knows about it too but since it started out in the county, it falls under Brett's jurisdiction. Plus, I think he wants to make sure we're extra safe."

"Well, I'm going to go get things started," Maggie said. "Why don't you just have a seat and I'll bring you some coffee?"

"We both know that's not going to happen," Ruby said. "I need to stay busy. I want to be busy."

"Okay," Maggie said. "Fair enough." She headed back to the kitchen and turned on the rest of the lights. She pulled a clean apron off of the hook on the wall and set about preparing the automatic donut machines for the first few batches of cake donuts. Ruby started her prep work for the boxed lunches and kept her head down as she worked.

A little while later, Maggie heard a knock at the back door. She wiped her hands off on the front of her apron and moved to open it.

"Hi, there," Brett said. "Is Ruby here? I'm sure she told you what happened this morning."

"Over here," Ruby called to him.

"Why don't you guys go use the office?" Maggie said. "Naomi will be here soon, and she can take over for you, Ruby."

Ruby nodded and led Brett into the office. Maggie busied herself with a batch of apple cider donuts while they spoke. She tried to focus on the batter in the mixer and her plans for the maple bacon donuts in a little while, but all she could think about was the situation with the mystery driver running around and following women in the middle of the night.

There was no doubt that something had happened to Ruby, but there was still so much that didn't make a lick of sense to her. Why was Ruby the only victim of the serial stalker who had felt safe enough to talk to law enforcement in person? Was it just because of her relationships with Brooks and

Brett that she felt safe enough to give her name and meet with them?

The cameras! In her concern with Ruby, she'd forgotten about the security cameras outside of the donut shop. She rushed to the office door and pointed to the laptop. "Brett! The cameras. We need to check the cameras to see if the driver is on there."

Brett moved out of her way and held his hand out to her over the desk. "Yes, it was the first thing I was going to mention when I was done talking with Ruby. If you want to take a look, go for it."

Ruby was quiet while Maggie opened up her laptop and turned the screen toward the two of them. She moved the mouse around to show the front cameras. With a few clicks, they watched the video from about an hour before. Maggie fast forwarded the video until they could see a pair of headlights. She slowed the video down and watched.

"That looks like my truck," Ruby said. She pointed to the screen. "I was headed in fast. Because the truck behind me was really pushing me."

"There's another set of headlights behind you," Brett said. "Slow that down a little bit, Maggie." She nodded and hit the mouse a few more times. They watched as the second truck sped in behind Ruby and turned sharply around the parking lot. The truck stopped in front of the front door, revved up the motor several times, and took off again down the road.

"Rewind that and see if you can stop it where we can see the driver," Brett told her.

Maggie complied and stopped the video when the driver came into view. "I think that's the best we're going to get," she told Brett, and handed him over the mouse. "See if you can get a better view."

Brett took the mouse from her and moved the picture back a few frames and then forward. He stopped when the grainy image of the driver came more clearly into view. "Here we go," he said.

"That doesn't look like a man in the driver's seat to me," Ruby said.

"No, it doesn't," Brett agreed.

"Whoever it is, they are wearing sunglasses and while it is still dark outside," Maggie said. She turned to Brett. "Does that remind you of something?"

"Yeah," he said. "It sure does."

CHAPTER TEN

Brett left with a copy of the video and headed back to his office. Maggie returned to work and said little as she made the last batch of apple cider donuts and started on the cinnamon rolls. Myra arrived at work and got busy icing everything from her perch on a stool where she could work without being on her feet for too long.

Maggie checked on Ruby from time to time and found her uninterested in talking about what had happened. When Naomi stepped in to take over the donut production, Maggie announced that she was going to take her first break. She picked up her phone from her office and headed out to the dining room. She grabbed a fresh cinnamon roll and a cinnamon latte, a habit she had picked up from spending so much time with Brett.

With her latte and her warm cinnamon roll, Maggie sat down in her usual booth and began scrolling through her phone. Curious, she opened up her news app and began searching around the area for other reports of vehicles stalking women at night.

Her phone alerted her to an incoming text message. She clicked on it and read a message from Brett.

"Went over the video from this morning and think we have enough for a partial identification of both the driver and the license plate," he wrote.

"That's wonderful," Maggie replied.

"It's also strange," he texted back. "It's quite clear that the driver of the truck from this morning is a woman."

Maggie thought back to the night she thought she had been followed coming back from Hunter Springs. "Could it maybe have been that same old man I thought was following me? He was a smaller guy," she suggested in her message back to him. "Maybe he was lying after all. He wore sunglasses, too."

"I'm headed over to question him," Brett said. "How is Ruby?"

"Stoic," Maggie replied. She clicked out of her

texting app and began scrolling through the rest of her phone while she ate her breakfast.

She remembered a few photos she'd taken of Wyatt that she wanted to have printed, and as she was scanning her photo gallery, she found the picture she'd taken at the grocery store. "Oh, wow," she said. She had caught a great close-up picture of Erin Johnson. It was a little blurry, but it was perfect for what she needed. Much better news than the selfie she'd thought she'd taken.

Never being so glad to have switched the camera around accidentally, she downloaded the photo to her phone memory and opened up a search engine in the browser. She clicked on the "photo search" tab and uploaded the photo to the website.

A second later, the pieces of the stalker mystery began to fall into place. Maggie scrolled through several newspaper articles and read, wide-eyed, accounts of wild claims of stalking vehicles, faceless intruders, even a campaign of threatening letters.

Each story had one thing in common: Erin Johnson's name and photo were front and center as the alleged victim and the person making the claims.

"I knew something was off," she said. She stood and dumped the remainder of her breakfast in the trash and headed to the kitchen. She stopped for a moment and surveyed the women working back there. She hesitated to say a word to any of them, including Ruby. Instead, she hastily announced that she needed to run a fast errand and headed out the door to her car.

She started up her car and drove to the end of the alley. She waited for a moment and searched for an address for Erin and then sent the articles and the photo to Brett in bulk.

She made it out of town and onto the highway before he reached her. "What are you doing?" he asked when he called.

"I'm headed out to the golf course between Dogwood Mountain and Hunter Springs," she told him. "I think it's a gated community, so I'm not sure I can get in there to see her."

"What are you going to do once you do, Maggie? Accuse her of staging this whole thing?"

"No," she said. "I'm just going to start by asking her what the heck is going on."

"Don't do anything until I get there," Brett ordered her. "I'm just a minute or two behind you."

Maggie set her phone safely on the passenger seat and headed for the pricey neighborhood surrounding a small lake and golf course about ten minutes from the town of Dogwood Mountain. She had rarely visited the place, and even as a child, the large houses had been homes to only the wealthiest people around town. She had even heard rumors that some old school country music stars from the Branson area had bought homes in the area, but she wasn't sure if that was true or mere speculation.

Either way, she wondered how Erin had managed to afford to live there. Any of the times Maggie had seen her, it had been in the middle of the work day and Erin had shown no evidence that she even had a job.

She reached the front gate to the neighborhood and sighed in relief to find it open. She sighed again when she spotted the sheriff's vehicle behind her. Brett followed her around through a few winding roads before she turned onto Payne Street. The house was located at the end of a large cul-de-sac.

Maggie noticed a dark green Dodge Ram pickup parked in the drive next to the house.

"That's the same make and model of the truck on the video from this morning," Brett whispered into her hair when he came up behind her. He took the lead and walked up to the front door.

Erin opened the door before either one of them could knock or ring the doorbell.

"Oh, Sheriff Mission, Maggie! I've been expecting the two of you," she announced. She was dressed in a long blue skirt and a polka dotted blouse, covered by a dress length frilly apron. "Lunch is just about ready."

"Lunch?" Brett asked her.

"Yes, lunch, silly! Please follow me," Erin said. She disappeared down a dark hallway.

"No, Ms. Johnson. We need to ask you a few questions," Brett hollered after her. "Please come back to the front door so we can talk." He moved Maggie behind him and unsnapped his gun holster.

"Just come back here and eat lunch," Erin hollered back.

"I don't smell any food cooking," Maggie said quietly.

"Neither do I," Brett said. "Stay here." He pulled his gun out of the holster and held it in front of him as he walked down the hallway.

Maggie waited about thirty seconds before she followed in Brett's footsteps. She moved down the long hallway past several rooms. She looked inside the first two rooms. Both rooms had ornate light fixtures, carpet, and windows, but no furniture. Stacks of moving boxes sat in the middle of each room.

Maggie walked toward the light at the end of the hallway and listened for a moment. "Please, Sheriff," she heard Erin say. "Please don't shoot us!"

"I'm not going to shoot anyone," Brett said. She heard a cautious edge in his voice. "Please, just have a seat at the table like we talked about. Maybe Miss Sharpe will join us for lunch after all." Maggie walked slowly further down the hall. As she walked, she could hear Brett mumbling in the radio receiver on his lapel.

"How are things going?" Maggie asked. She walked past another empty room with a fireplace on one end and into the large, sunny kitchen. She gasped when she saw the large spread for lunch laid out on mismatched China platters. The food was tiny, perfectly formed, and plastic. The table was set with tiny doll plates and tea cups. Erin was seated at the head with a large, very real knife in her hand.

Brett stood about five feet from her. His gun was still in his hand, but for the moment, the barrel was pointed down at the floor.

"What's going on in here?" Maggie asked carefully.

"I couldn't wait for you to ask," Erin said brightly. "I've been wanting to talk to you about something."

"Talk to me?" Maggie asked carefully. She glanced at Brett, who nodded slightly at her. "What do you want to talk about?"

"I want you to tell me why you think it's okay to

steal my dream building right out from underneath me."

"What do you mean?" Maggie asked. "What building?" She looked around the room again, this time noticing more dolls. It registered to her what Erin was talking about before she had the chance to reply.

"You are the fourth person to have stolen from me. That old gas station was perfect for my doll business. With the kitchen inside, I could have hosted a tea service for all my customers, but no. Instead, you swoop in and take it right out from underneath me, just like the others did."

"Miss Johnson, what are you talking about?" Brett asked, at the ready.

"Why don't you sit down for some lunch and your girlfriend here can tell you all about it? Maybe this time, someone will listen to me."

"Erin," Maggie began. She took a step closer to try to convince the woman she wasn't a threat. "I didn't mean to take anything from anyone. I loved the old filling station so much and wanted it for my business, too. I'm sorry it worked out the way it did for you. Maybe there is another place close by that will work."

Brett cleared his throat and Erin glared in his direction.

"That's what all the others said, too. One person even offered to help me find a new place using their own realtor. Only once they found out I was trying to open a doll business, they ditched me. Just because they don't want a business like mine in their precious little town."

As Maggie looked around the room again, she had to admit that dolls were pretty creepy, but Erin and how far she'd taken this was worse.

"I'd like to help you," Maggie said. "But I have to admit that I'm not feeling very safe here right now."

Erin nodded. "It isn't safe anywhere," she whispered.

"Do you usually tell the police when bad stuff happens?" Maggie asked her. A picture was starting to form in her mind about the serial stalker and the other articles she had read just an hour before.

"I do, but no one wants to take me seriously," Erin said. "Not with the stalking and not with my business."

"Hey, Erin," Maggie said cheerfully. She cast a meaningful look at Brett. "Why don't you tell me more about your doll business?" She wanted to know more about the stalking and really couldn't care less about the business, but she got the feeling that talking about it would make Erin more comfortable.

Maggie watched the woman's face almost transform into a six-year-old little girl's as she spoke.

"My whole life I loved dolls. I used to play with my grandmother's dolls when I was a kid. She had a doll hospital business and ever since then, I knew what I wanted to do with my life. Except the problem is, no one takes me seriously. They all think my dolls are weird and I'm sick of it."

"Have you been trying to get even with the people that you feel stole from you?" Maggie asked.

"That's not how it started," Erin said, running her finger over the knife. "But you seem awfully happy that you got the filling station."

Maggie took a deep breath. "I am happy. I love it there, but that doesn't mean I'm glad you don't have it. Can you tell me anything about the stalking you mentioned earlier?" She hoped her plan would work.

Erin looked up and nodded her head. "Someone followed me late one night. I'd had a bad day looking for locations for my business and I couldn't sleep, so I went out for a drive. A man was following me, and when I pulled over to let him pass, he slowed down and got out, coming toward me. I called the police, but no one believed what I had to say because of old reports about things I supposedly did."

"Are you saying you didn't do the things in all those reports?" Maggie asked.

"No, I definitely did things to the people that needed it. Some people just deserve to be put in their place. I got so mad no one believed me and then, on top of that, I kept losing my dream spots. I decided to scare people like I got scared. It worked on me, and I figured it would work on them, too. I wanted them to feel like I did when I realized that my dreams were being squashed again."

"You said you called the police about being followed?" Maggie asked, hoping Brett would join in on the conversation.

"I did call them," Erin said. "Like I said, they didn't think I was reliable."

"If you're talking about Dogwood Mountain police, it wasn't that anyone thought you were unreliable,

tt's that you didn't even tell us your name," Brett said quietly. "We can't help if we don't know who we're talking to."

"Because when I tell the police who I am, they look me up and they stop believing what I am trying to tell them," Erin said. "It's happened before in other towns."

Brett sighed. "I understand, but if you did things before to cause trouble, then that sort of stuff follows you around. I know you just want to open your business, but scaring the people who got a building before you did isn't the way to do it."

"Erin, you scared me and a lot of other people in my life and probably plenty more than that based on what you've said already. You know it's not okay to drive around and frighten people, right?"

"No more than it's okay for you to have stolen my dream building. That old filling station was perfect for me, and I don't care how good it is for you. That place was mine. It should have been mine."

Erin's head dropped again. She moved the knife between her hands. "It's not like I killed anyone, jeez. I just needed people to realize that they can't keep messing with me and getting away with it."

Maggie moved closer to the end of the table. She knelt on the floor and gripped the chair next to Erin's. "Why are you holding the knife like that?" she asked quietly, trying to ignore the glare from Brett. She knew he'd wanted her to back away, but she couldn't help it.

"Because now that I'm in the hot seat, I'm feeling

like maybe killing someone is the right idea," Erin said. A single tear traced down her cheek. "I can't go to jail. I'll never open my business that way."

Maggie lunged forward slightly and wrapped her hand around the handle of the knife. "Yes, that's right. You need to open your business. You can't go to jail," she said. "Everyone makes mistakes." She pulled the knife away from Erin's hands. The woman resisted for a moment and then gave it up. Maggie stood quickly and carried the knife to the sink.

Footsteps filled the hallway. Two deputies from the sheriff's department arrived, followed by a pair of paramedics. Maggie stood over the sink and breathed deeply. She fought the urge to hyperventilate and let go of the knife. It clattered to the bottom of the sink.

CHAPTER ELEVEN

"I think we're going to have to start buying bacon in bulk," Naomi announced the next morning. She carried an empty tray that had once been filled with maple bacon donuts to the sink.

"I've looked into that," Maggie said. "That's what I was doing the day I ran into Erin at the grocery store."

"Was that also the day you ran into Preston, that weird guy from the old bookstore?" Naomi asked. "I wonder if she was going to try to frame him for the stalking?"

Maggie shrugged. "Who knows? I mean, I can't say that I'd mind if he wasn't around…"

"Maggie!" Ruby scolded her. "You'd better be careful what you say."

"Well, if what you guys have told me is true, I think Preston is a big jerk and that Erin woman probably deserves to be in trouble for what she did. I mean, can you imagine if the old filling station actually became a doll shop? How creepy would that be?" Naomi shuddered. "Dolls are the worst."

"I think that if this is how she reacted to things, it's probably best that she doesn't run a business. I guess the woman she was with that day at the store was supposed to go into business with her," Maggie said. "Brett told me she went running for the hills."

Ruby chuckled. "I bet she did. The worst part about Erin was that she had to start bringing other people into her lie to make it seem more true."

"Do you think there ever was a stalker?" Myra asked her. "I heard the only reason she knew about your situation was because she heard it over the scanner. I bet that's why she was wearing sunglasses when she followed Ruby. Like she was trying to find another person to blame for what she was doing herself."

"Brett says that he thinks so, at some point," Maggie said. "I mean, look at me the night I came back home from Hunter Springs and thought someone was following me. It was an innocent mistake. Perhaps she had the same kind of experience and somehow created the idea to do it to other people who she believed had wronged her in some way. Unfortunately, I think things played out in all the wrong ways for her."

"I don't know. I guess you're right about her running a business, though," Myra said. "I just can't believe how she really felt like everyone else was to blame for her missing out on a location. I hate to say it, but maybe it's better off it happened the way it did."

"I can't believe she really thought she was going to hurt us," Maggie said. "I mean Brett was right there. Who acts that way in front of the police?"

Myra laughed. "From what I heard, Maggie, you were the one who saved the day. It wasn't Brett who took that knife away, was it?"

She shook her head. "I was closer to her and less of a threat. Even if she was upset with me for getting the old filling station, Brett is the official and had a weapon, too. That automatically makes me less frightening to a person in her situation."

Ruby had said little since the woman had been caught red-handed. She pointed to the empty bacon donut tray. "How long did those donuts last?" she asked, changing the subject back to something more pleasant.

"Fifteen minutes," Naomi said. She pushed the tray into the hot, soapy water in the sink and began cleaning it. "How long before the next batch is ready?"

"Maybe twenty minutes," Maggie added. "I think we need to see what we can do about streamlining the process. These donuts take too long to produce in large batches."

"Darn that kid of yours," Myra said from the corner. She was seated on a stool close to the door to the cooler. "He just had to come up with a bestselling idea!"

"Speaking of kids, how are you feeling today?" Maggie asked her. "You are getting so close to your due date."

"Same old, same old," Myra said. "Except this little one is moving around like she's kicking the soccer ball into the goal. She's definitely active today!"

"It's all that bacon," Orson grumbled from the corner. "My grandmother used to tell me that children in her day weren't allowed to have bacon. It was considered too rich for them."

"What do you expect? Your grandmother's generation probably thought showing their ankles was scandalous," Naomi said.

"Would that have been before or after the wagon train rolled on in to Oklahoma?" Myra teased.

"That's it," Orson said. He set down his donut tray and headed straight for the kitchen door. "You ladies can handle things all by yourselves. I'm taking a break and having a cup of coffee."

"It's not even eight o'clock and you're going on break?" Ruby called after him.

"You heard me," Orson called back through the swinging door. "And let's get busy with those maple bacon donuts! There is a crowd out here demanding more!" Loud laughter from the customers in the dining room followed.

"One day, I am going to throw that man outside by his big ears," Maggie said.

"You won't do any such thing," Ruby said. "You'll keep him here as long as he is willing to be here."

"And who said he has big ears?" Naomi said. "I think Orson has nice ears. Just like he has nice silver hair."

"Thank you, doll," Orson called back from the lobby area. "You're my new favorite."

Ruby nodded her head. "That's why she said he had big ears," she whispered.

"I get it now," Naomi said, laughing.

"Orson is an ornery old man," Myra said. She shifted on her stool. She looked up at Maggie. "Whenever the maple bacon donuts are ready, I have a double batch of icing here for them. I just don't feel like getting up right now."

"I can't imagine why," Ruby said. "I understand the desire to stay busy working for as long as you can, but I think you've earned a long break."

"Especially before the baby comes," Maggie chimed in. "Once she's here, you won't know a moment's rest for a few months."

"You sound like the woman at the grocery store when I went by yesterday to pick up a few extra things," Myra said. "I want to make sure I have dinners for a few weeks after I have the baby."

"Dinners? Are you serious? You do know you are going to get sick of the pampering you will be getting once she gets here, right?" Maggie asked her. "I've even spoken with Gretchen about renting out a couple of rooms from her at Dogwood House for Brooks's family. And she has agreed to keep two rooms on hold starting this weekend."

"That's very kind of her," Myra said. "But the world isn't going to stop just because I'm having a baby."

"Hey, Myra," Naomi said from the prep table,

where she assisted Ruby with the day's boxed lunches.

"You might as well accept the fact that you're not just having a baby; we're all having a baby."

"I guess you're right," Myra said. She made a face and hugged her large belly. "That's the way things are with Wyatt, too."

"Speaking of Wyatt," Ruby said. "I wonder how he's going to take having another baby around."

"He's going to be great," Maggie said with certainty.

"How come you never had another one, Maggie?" Josie posed the question from the doorway to the store room.

"Josie," Naomi said in a half-whisper. "I don't think that's an appropriate question."

Josie's face paled and her hand went to her mouth. "Oh, I am sorry," she said. "I just figured it was a topic of conversation. I didn't think about it that way. Like, I would never ask Ruby why she never had kids."

"How do you know I never had kids?" Ruby said. "As a matter of fact, I have eight kids in a remote village in Scotland."

Josie's eyes widened. "You do? You have eight kids? Why are they in Scotland?"

Ruby chuckled and shook her head. "I don't have any kids of my own," she said. "And to answer your question, I was always too busy with my career. I actually sponsor a few kids in a small village in Scotland, so there is some truth to what I said."

"And as to why I never had any more than Bradley, he was more than enough to handle." Maggie drew in a deep breath. She noticed a smirk form on Josie's face. "I couldn't imagine having more than one after Bradley and his wild ways."

"Poor Bradley," Ruby shook her head but was grinning as she spoke.

"Hey, you guys," Myra called from her seat. "I think we have a problem with the cooler."

"What problem would that be?" Ruby asked. She headed for the cooler and opened the door. "Everything looks okay, and it's holding the right temperature."

"No, I think there is some kind of a leak," Myra said. She held her belly in her arms and looked around on the floor beneath her stool. "There's a puddle of water here now."

"I don't know if that's from the cooler," Ruby said. "Let me take a look outside."

"Hey, Ruby," Maggie said. She picked up a towel

and headed for the cooler. "I don't think that's going to be necessary."

"Why not?" Myra asked. "Shouldn't we figure out if the cooler has a leak? The last thing we need is a cooler on the fritz."

"Because it isn't the cooler that's leaking," Maggie said. "You are."

"Josie, go quietly and get Orson from the front," Maggie said. "Tell him that we are going to need to get a ride to the hospital."

"I'm going to go call the new chief of police," Ruby said.

"Oh," Myra said. She doubled over. "This baby is kicking the dickens out of me!"

"That's not the baby kicking," Maggie said. "That's the baby coming! And the last time it happened was just about six minutes ago."

The swinging door flew open, and Orson appeared in the kitchen, red-faced and eager. "Are we having a baby?"

"We are," Myra said. "Now, help me to the car so we can get to the hospital. I don't want to have a baby in a donut shop."

CHAPTER TWELVE

Maggie woke to a bird singing outside of her bedroom window early the following morning. There would be no donuts to make, no donut shop to open for the day. Instead, she planned to visit a large home on the other side of town bearing gifts for a new baby.

She showered and dressed to formally meet the baby and check in on the new parents. Her phone rang twenty minutes before she planned to leave.

"I wondered if you might like to go over to the Macklin house together?" Brett asked her. "I have taken the day off and told my secretary not to bother me unless there is a terrorist attack."

"Sure." Maggie smiled. "I was planning on going over there anyway, so this is perfect." She hung up her phone and headed back to the bathroom for another check of her hair and makeup.

Brett arrived in his vintage muscle car a few minutes later. Maggie grabbed a jacket when she headed out the back door to meet him. Brett got out of the driver's side and moved around to open the passenger door for her. She glanced at the backseat, which was filled with several pink gift bags.

"Did you go shopping?"

Brett returned to his seat and grinned. He leaned in and pecked her playfully on the lips. "I'm so excited to meet her."

"I'm glad we gave them the privacy at the hospital yesterday, but it's time. I can barely wait," Maggie agreed.

They drove quickly to the Macklin' house. Maggie pulled up the seat and reached in for as many of the gift bags as she could carry. Brett followed suit. They approached the front door. Brooks opened it with a flourish before Brett could knock.

"Welcome," Brooks whispered. "The baby just fell asleep in Myra's arms."

"We'll be quiet," Maggie said. She kissed Brooks on the cheek as she passed him.

Myra was seated in the rocking chair in the living room. She held a small pink bundle in her lap.

Maggie set the gift bags down and moved to stand over her. "How precious," she whispered. She hugged her from the side.

"She's so wonderful," Myra said, teary-eyed.

Maggie took a seat on the couch across from her. "I still can't believe how fast she came."

Myra nodded. "You and me both," she said. "My doctor said it'd been a while since she'd seen anything like it."

"So, I gotta know. What's her name?" Brett asked.

"Yes! I've been waiting so long to hear," Maggie said eagerly.

Myra exchanged a sweet smile with Brooks and sat forward a little in her rocking chair. "Funny you should ask. We just settled on her name this morning."

"Okay, so, what is it?" Maggie couldn't contain herself.

"We decided to name her Lexington Elizabeth Macklin, but we'll call her Lexi," Myra explained.

"You're the first to hear her full name," Brooks said.

"Right." Myra nodded. "So far, Orson has just heard us calling her baby girl."

"And how has Orson been with her?" Maggie asked. Myra stood up and carefully laid the baby girl in her arms. The baby fussed for a second and then snuggled closer.

"That's a beautiful picture," Brett leaned over her and said. Maggie looked up at him and simply smiled.

"Orson is the best grandpa either of us could have hoped for," Brooks said.

"This grandpa would like to hear the name of his granddaughter, if you two have finally made up your minds," Orson said as he walked into the living room.

"We were just discussing that," Brooks said.

"And?" Orson asked. He moved over to where Maggie was seated with the small baby girl and lovingly touched her small head.

"Well, then. Meet Lexi Elizabeth," Myra said.

"Lexi," Orson said quietly.

Brooks moved next to him and placed an arm around Orson's thin shoulders. "Her full name is Lexington Elizabeth Macklin. We decided to name her after the man who has been there for us since the moment we met him and who will continue to be there for our daughter."

Maggie watched carefully, not quite understanding. "Who is she named after?"

"Lexington is Orson's middle name," Myra whispered and pointed to Orson. "We wanted to remind him just how important he is to our family."

Maggie couldn't hold back the happy tears as she gently handed the baby up to Orson. He reached down and took her in his arms. "Hello, little Lexi," he whispered. Tears rolled down his weathered face. "I'm your grandpa, but you can call me 'Papa.'"

If you enjoyed One of Those Glaze, check out the next book in the series, None the Riser, today!

AUTHOR'S NOTE

I'd love to hear your thoughts on my books, the storylines, and anything else that you'd like to comment on—reader feedback is very important to me. My contact information, along with some other helpful links, is listed on the next page. If you'd like to be on my list of "folks to contact" with updates, release and sales notifications, etc.… just shoot me an email and let me know. Thanks for reading!

Also…

… if you're looking for more great reads, Summer Prescott Books publishes several popular series by outstanding Cozy Mystery authors.

CONTACT SUMMER PRESCOTT BOOKS PUBLISHING

Blog and Book Catalog: http://summerprescottbooks.com
Email: summer.prescott.cozies@gmail.com

And…be sure to check out the Summer Prescott Cozy Mysteries fan page and Summer Prescott Books Publishing Page on Facebook – let's be friends!

To sign up for our fun and exciting newsletter, which will give you opportunities to win prizes and swag, enter contests, and be the first to know about New Releases, click here: http://summerprescottbooks.com

Made in United States
North Haven, CT
15 March 2023

34102866R00065